My G-r-r-r-reat Uncle Tiger

James Riordan

Illustrated by Alex Ayliffe

PEACHTREE
ATLANTA

To Perry
JR

To Jessica
AA

Published by
PEACHTREE PUBLISHING COMPANY INC.
1700 Chattahoochee Avenue
Atlanta, Georgia 30318-2112
www.peachtree-online.com

Text © 1995 by James Riordan
Illustrations © 1995 by Alex Ayliffe

First trade paperback edition published in September 2000.
First published by Orchard Books in Great Britain in March 1995.

Printed in May 2019 in China
10 9 8 7 6 5 4 3 (trade paperback)
10 9 8 7 6 5 (hardcover)

HC ISBN: 978-1-56145-110-4
PB ISBN: 978-1-56145-228-6

Library of Congress Cataloging-in-Publication Data

Riordan, James.
My g-r-r-reat uncle tiger / by James Riordan : illustrated by Alex Ayliffe. -- 1st U.S. ed.
p. cm.
Summary: When Marmaduke the cat sees a picture of a tiger, he decides they must be related and sets off with his cat friends to find his great uncle tiger at the zoo.
ISBN 1-56145-110-X (hc)
[1. Cats--Fiction. 2. Tigers--Fiction.] I. Ayliffe, Alex, ill. II. Title.
PZ7.R487My 1995 95-13109
[E] -- dc20 CIP
AC

The house where Marmaduke lived was full of cats.

Downstairs lived Billy who hunted mice
and chased birds.

Upstairs, with a bed all
to herself, was Bertha.

Above her lived Matilda with her kitten Smudger.

And right at the top of the house was Albert, the wise old attic cat. From his window, he could see for miles around, and he knew all there was to know about everything.

One evening Marmaduke was going through the garbage cans outside the house when, among the fishtails and old bones, he found a book full of pictures. "Bless my marmalade socks," he exclaimed.

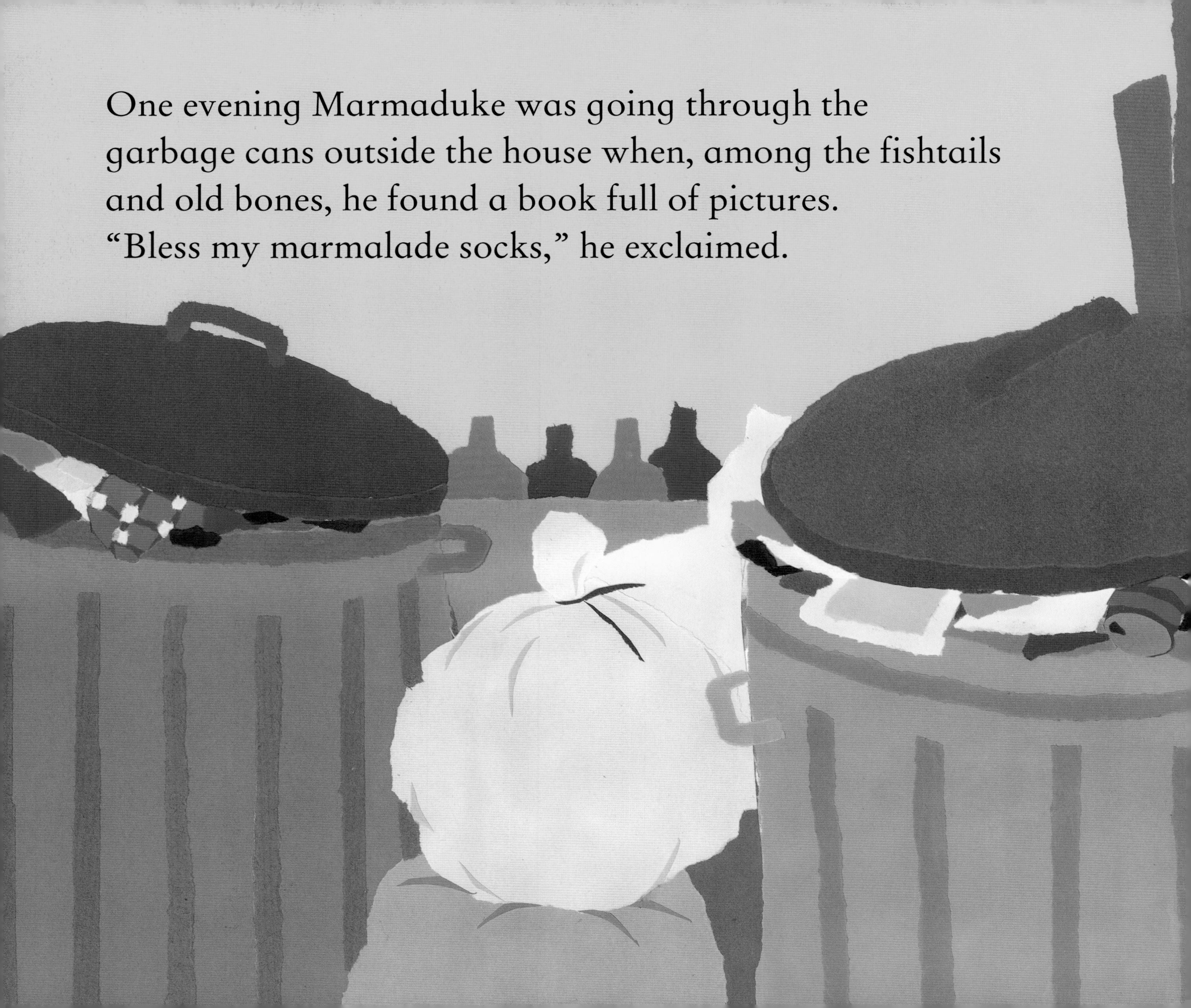

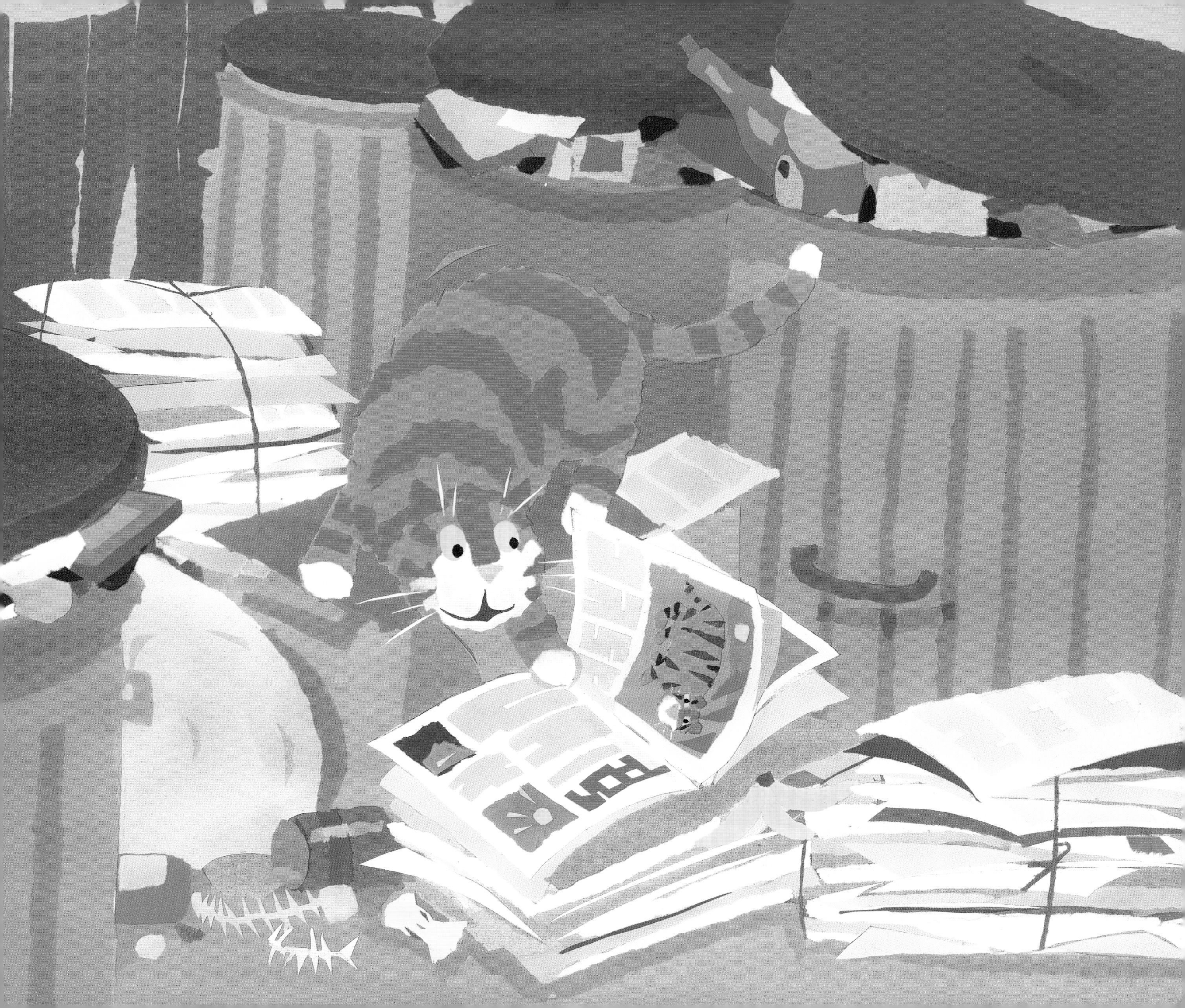

Marmaduke looked closer.
"A t-i-g-e-r! Well I never. Look at those yellow eyes and spiky whiskers. And he's got a long furry tail that curls like mine. And marmalade stripes — just like me. We must be related."

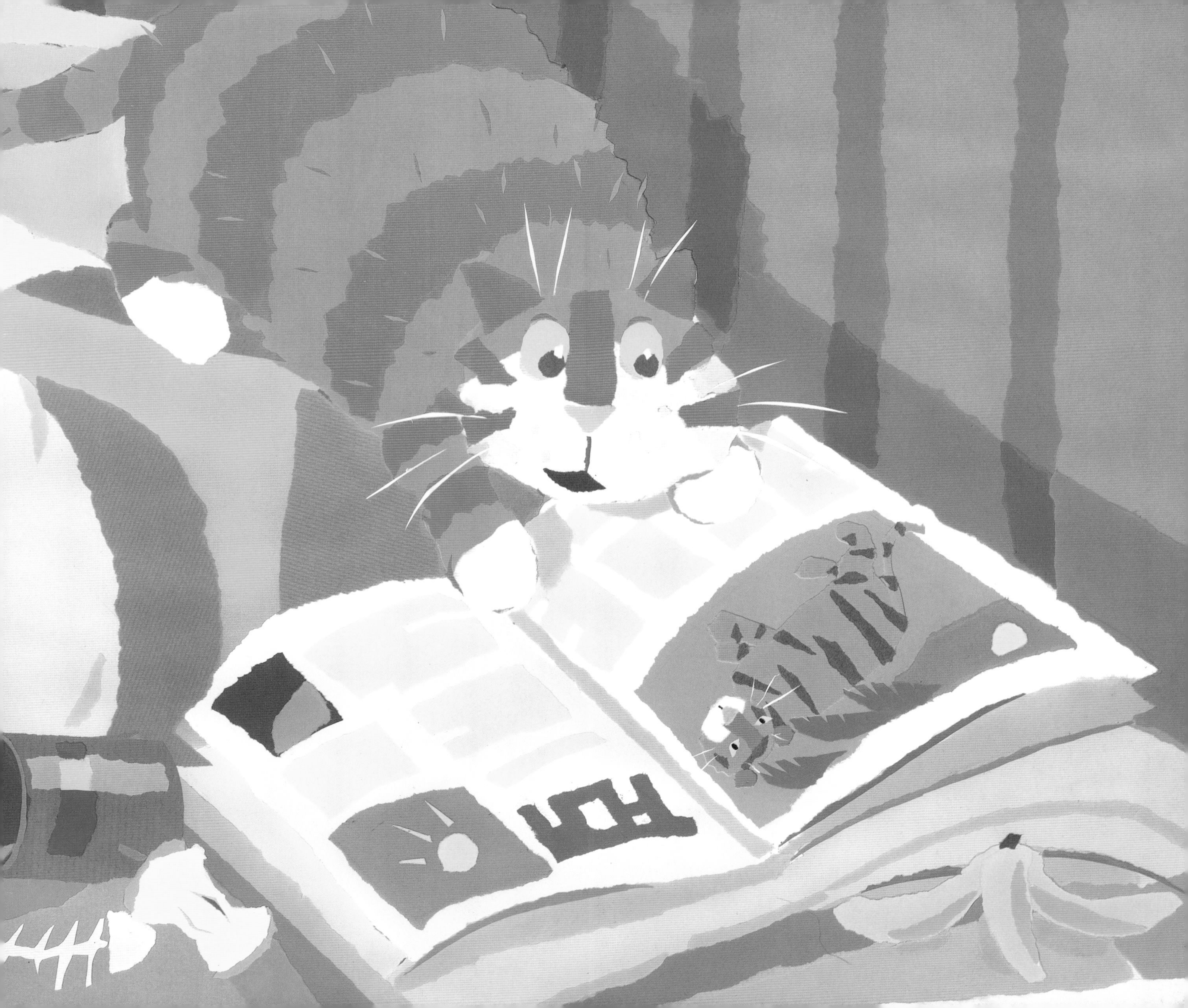

Every night the cats gathered on the rooftop to talk about the day's events. That evening Marmaduke couldn't wait to tell them his news, and he came across the roof with his nose held high and swishing his tail grandly.

And before any of the other cats were able
to say anything, Marmaduke began to
boast about his "uncle" tiger.

Little Smudger was very impressed. "Where does your great uncle tiger live? Can we meet him? Please?" he asked Marmaduke.

But it was wise old Albert who answered. "There are tigers at the zoo. I've seen them from my window. We could all go and see Marmaduke's uncle tiger."

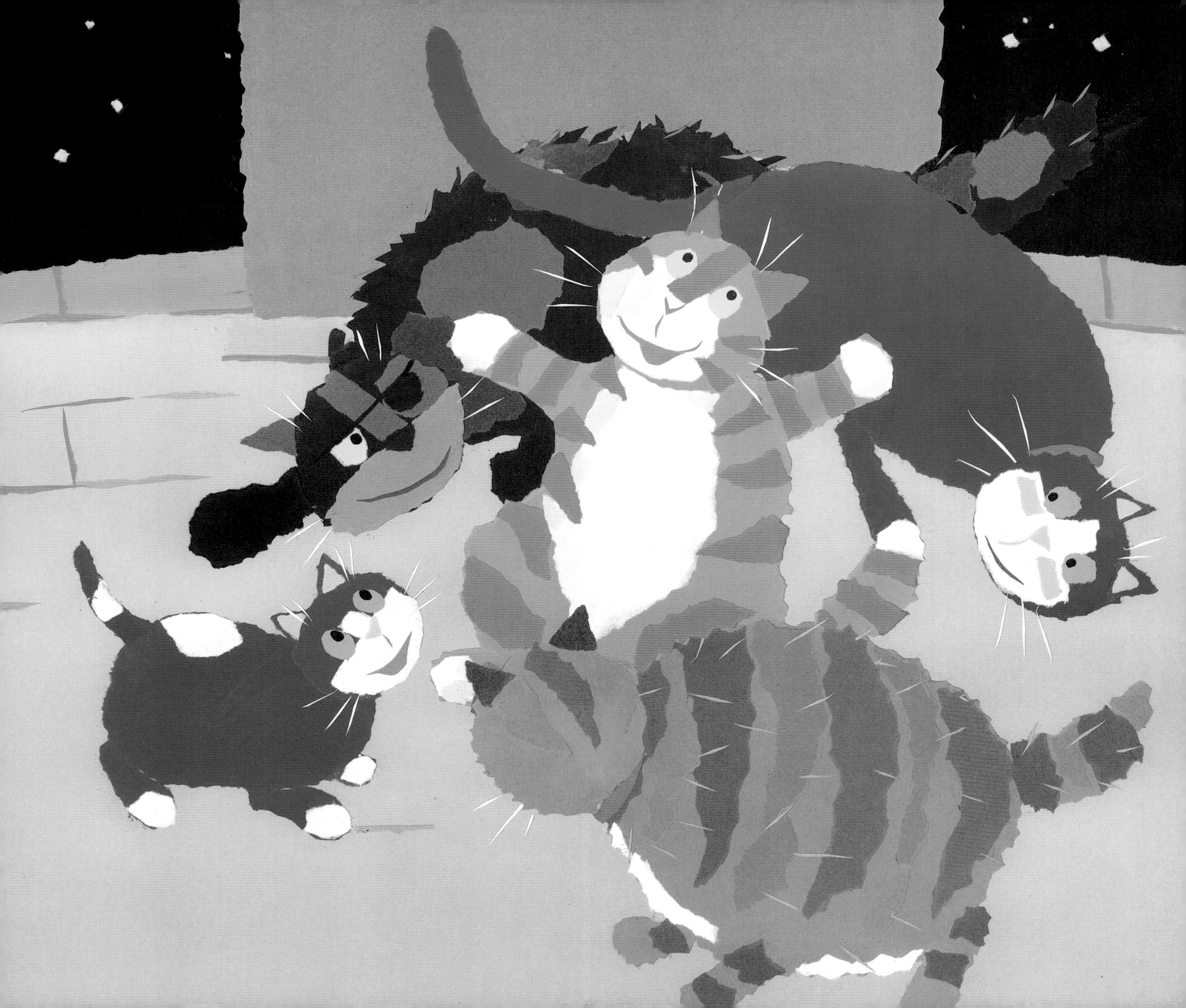

So first thing next morning the cats set off.

They tiptoed over rooftops, and filed across alleyways . . .

. . . and finally they squeezed through a hole in a high green fence, and there they were, inside the zoo.

"You go first," said Matilda to Marmaduke. "You know what he looks like."

"Oh, you won't have trouble spotting him," said Marmaduke. "He's the very fiercest, the very grandest and wisest of cats in the whole park. Follow me."

"Just look at that!" cried Smudger. Everyone stopped. "What's that huge animal climbing out of the water? That must be your uncle."

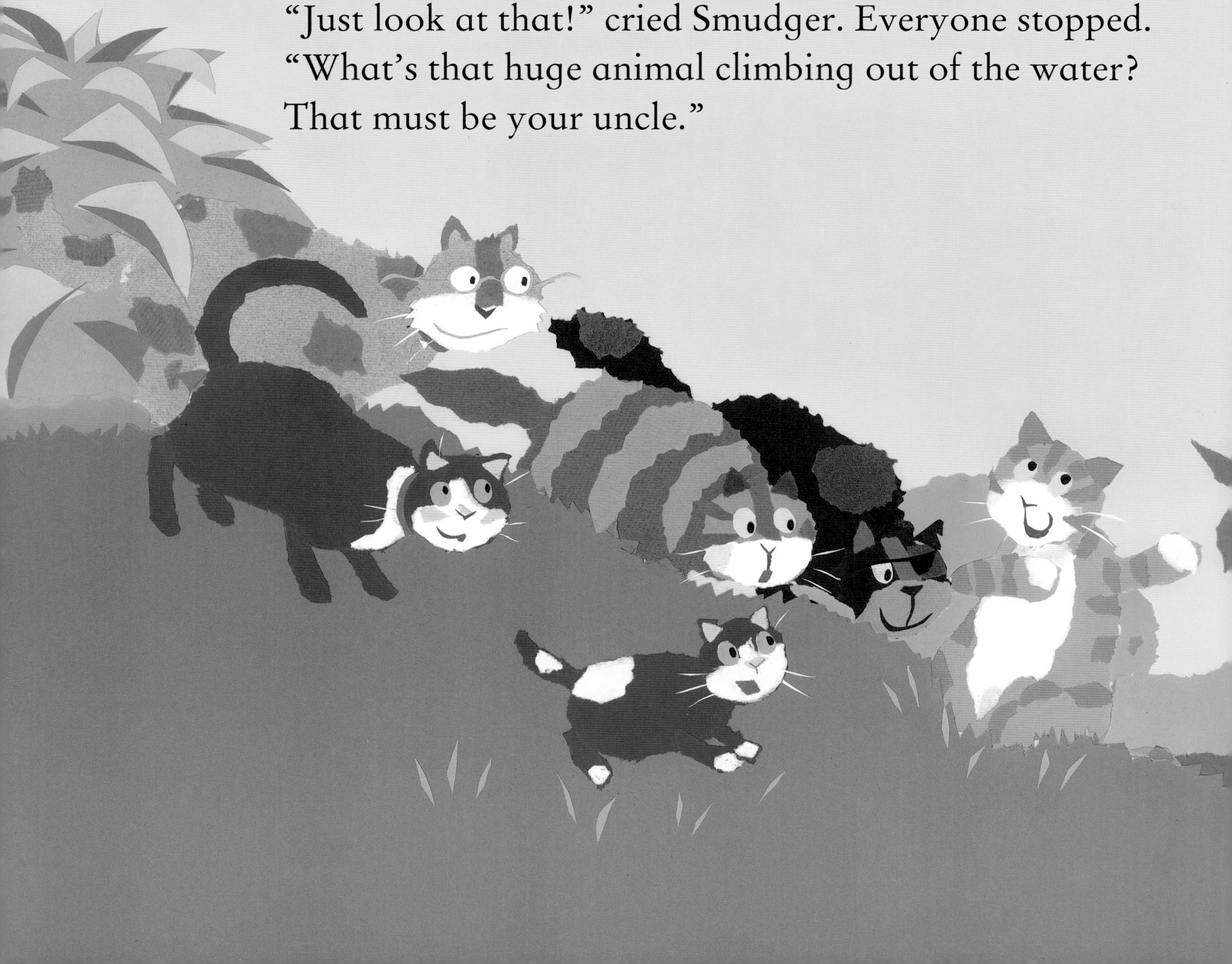

"What? That ugly fat frog!" scoffed Marmaduke.
"No, no, no. That's a hippo," said Albert wisely.
"Tigers are orange and furry," said Marmaduke.
"Come on!"

So on they went, past birds and animals of every shape and color.

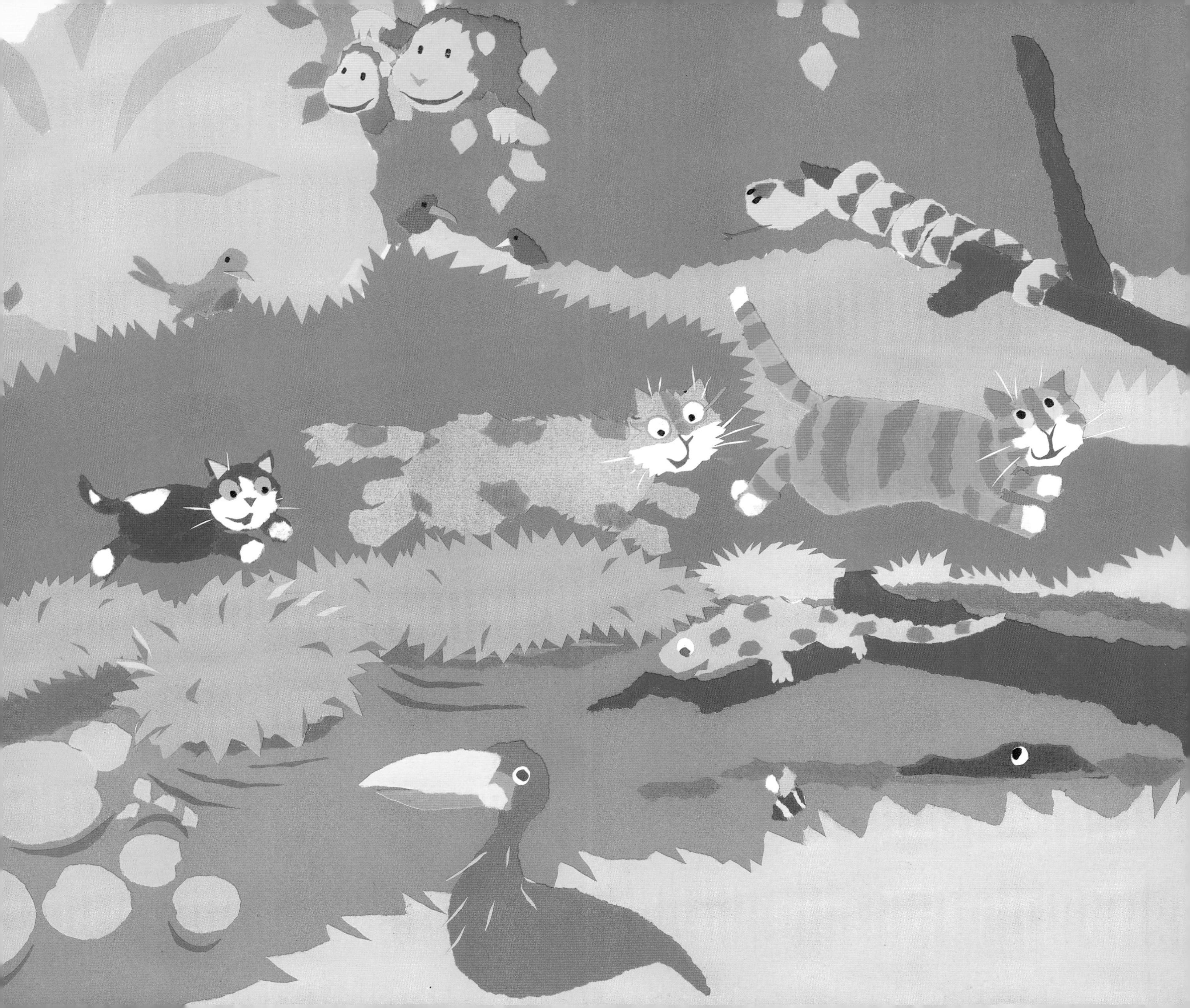

All of a sudden Smudger stopped again. "There's an orange and furry animal. Just look at him peering over the treetops. That's your uncle for sure."

"No, no, no," said Albert with a deep laugh. "That lofty beanpole is a giraffe."

"Besides," said Marmaduke. "Tigers have stripes."

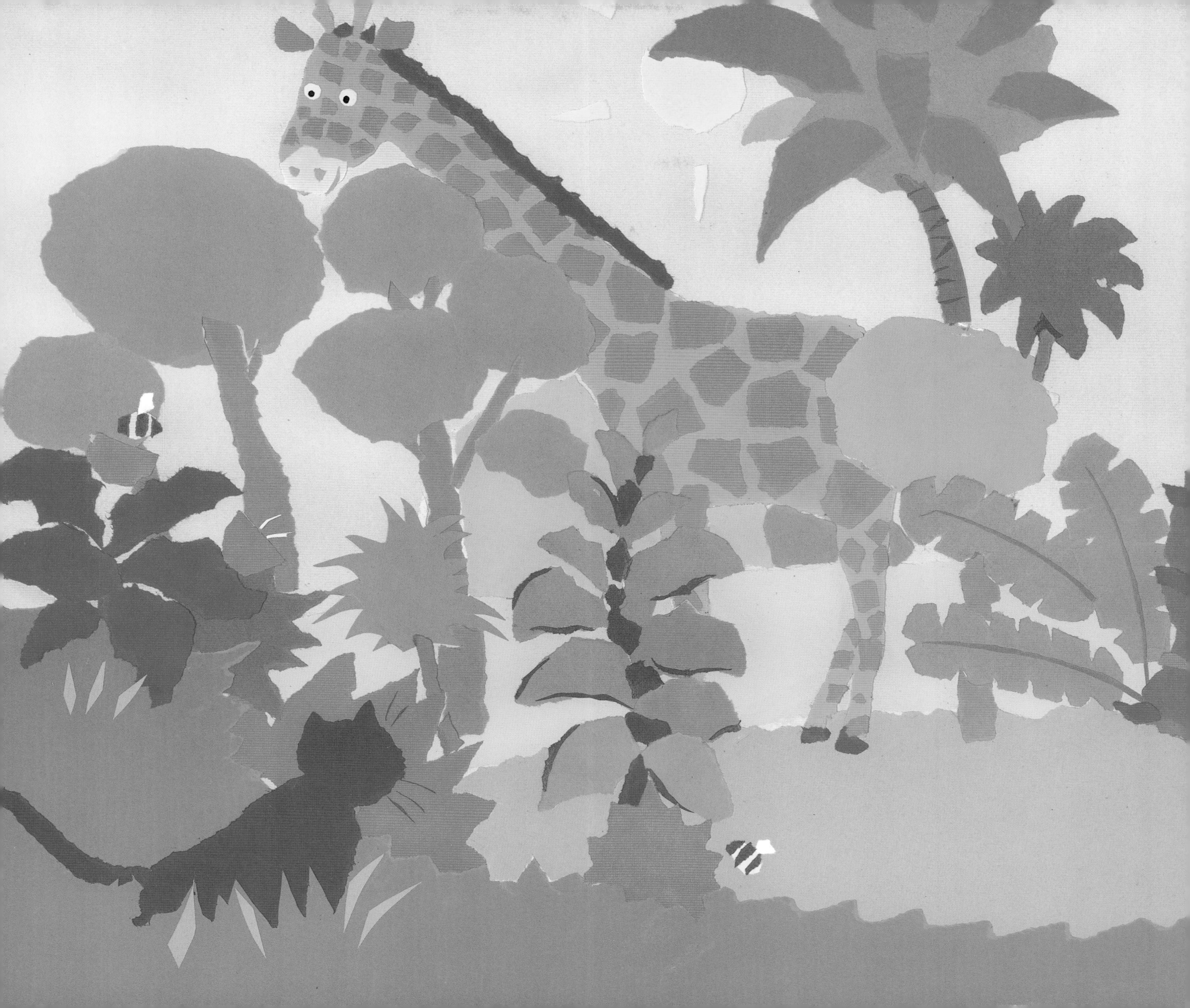

At last the cats reached the largest, most fearsome cat they had ever set eyes on. His yellow eyes gleamed wickedly, his white whiskers twitched, his long tail swished from side to side, and his great furry body was striped in orange and black from top to toe.

"There he is. That's him — that's my uncle!"
shouted Marmaduke.

Marmaduke walked boldly toward the tiger. But as he got closer his knees began to wobble. In real life his fierce great uncle looked rather scary.
"Er, hello, er, uncle," he said. "I've brought some friends to meet . . ."

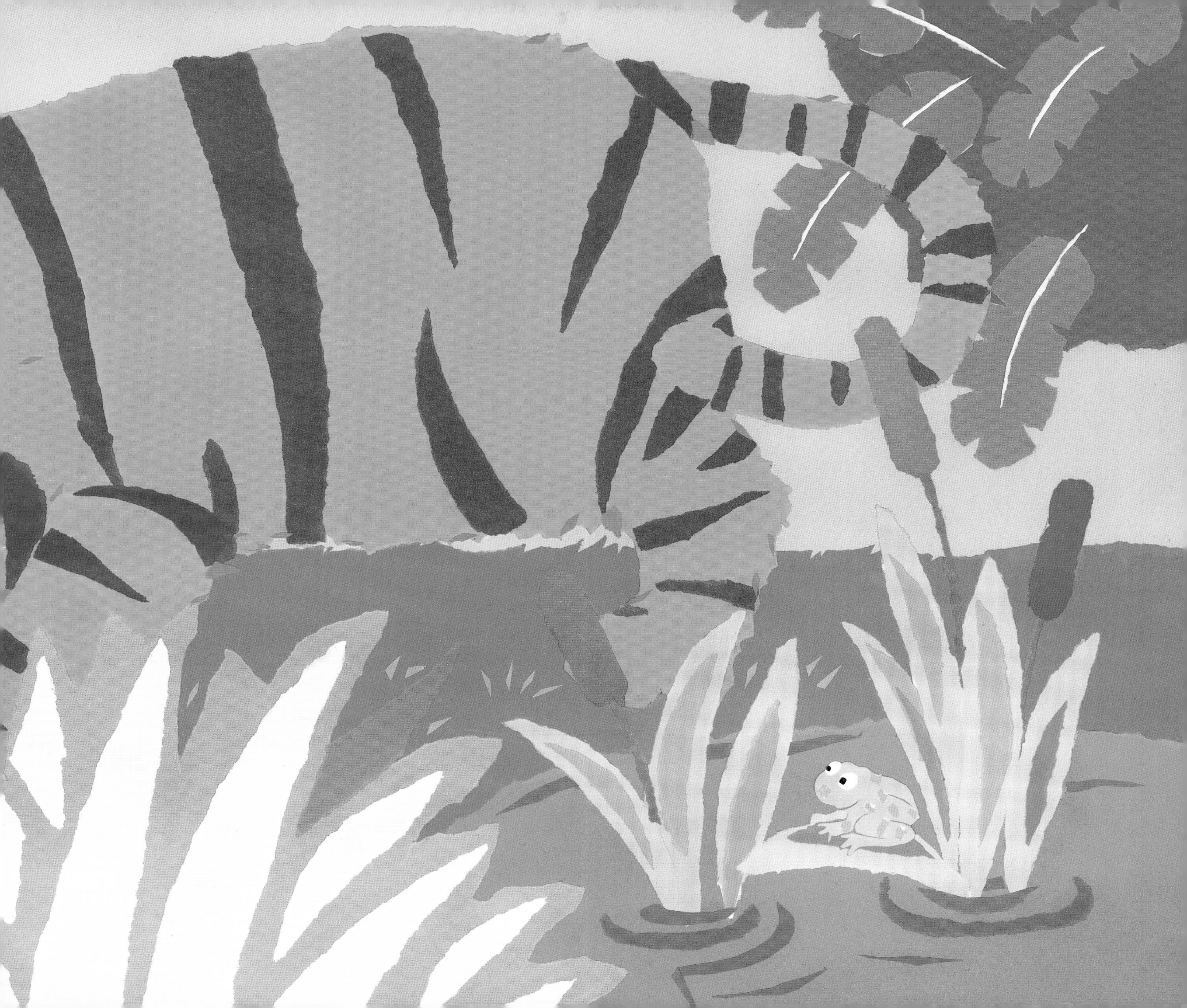

The tiger opened his great jaws to reveal two rows of big white teeth.

Grr-grr-grrr-

"GRRR-RRR--RRR-EEETINGS," said the tiger.

But Marmaduke did not hear his uncle tiger's words, nor did the other cats. Up they leapt and took to their heels for dear life.

Marmaduke was far ahead
of his friends, running for
all he was worth.

And never again did he boast
about his great uncle tiger.